# The Guts of a Mackerel

## Clare Reddaway

First published December 2021

Published in the UK by Fly on the Wall Press

56 High Lea Rd

New Mills

Derbyshire

SK22 3DP

www.flyonthewallpress.co.uk

ISBN: 978-1-913211-54-7

Supported using public funding by

**ARTS COUNCIL ENGLAND**

LOTTERY FUNDED

*For Auriol*

Eve was putting on mascara in the cottage bathroom. It was her good mascara, the *Maybelline Great Lash* she'd bought after saving her pocket money for weeks. It was hard enough when the mirror was the size of a handkerchief and hung far too high but she was blinking down on the wand, a trick she'd read about in *Just Seventeen* and the wand was especially big. It was supposed to make her eyelashes double thickness but instead it was clotting and sticking and every time she actually blinked, because she had to, the mascara fell off her eyelashes onto her cheeks so she looked like a clown but not in a good way, not like Adam Ant whose eyes were smoking. She had to look her best. He hadn't seen her for months and months and she'd definitely improved. Now the twins were bursting in and sticking out their tongues at her. One of them had some seaweed and was thwacking her ankles with it – her ankles would stink.

"Mum! They won't leave me alone!"

"Can you make up the bunk beds?"

Which was not the answer she wanted because no, she couldn't make up the bunk beds, she couldn't unpack, she couldn't stack the tins they'd brought, she couldn't do anything, because she had to, *had to*, see Liam right now. He didn't know she was here, didn't know they were even in Ireland, it was a big surprise. And now Mum wanted help.

"Piss off," she said to the Big Twin, pinching his wrist, not hard but hard enough to make him back away. She slid

5

out of the bathroom into the kitchen and was at the back door when the Small Twin saw her. He was about to shout but she put her finger to her lips – shuuusssshhhh! – and winked. He went pink with delight. A secret! And Eve was out.

She set off down the road to Liam's house. She'd got on her denim cut offs and her new wedges. She'd brushed her best plum frosted eye shadow onto her eyelids and she'd sprayed herself with Charlie, a present from her best friend Becca at her last birthday.

Butterflies were turning somersaults in her tummy. She hadn't seen Liam since last summer. They'd sent each other letters of course and she'd taken his into school to show Becca in triumph because a letter from a boy was big news, even if the letter was really short and the spelling was shocking. Last summer they'd spent almost every day of the holiday together, from when Eve's family had first arrived. They'd sat on the beach and they'd talked, properly talked, about their lives, their dreams, their futures. He'd held her hand and when she had to go because the holiday was over, he'd kissed her on her cheek. She hadn't washed the cheek for days, until the twins were flicking baked beans around at tea and one had hit her full in the face and it was either washing or living with a weird orange smear for the rest of her life. Liam was all she'd been thinking about since Dad said they were coming over for Easter. They'd have two and a half whole weeks!

She turned the corner and there was his house: square, painted white with a green door, an old Ford Escort with red Irish numberplates parked outside. It was all she could do not to run, but she forced herself to stroll, as though the idea of paying a call on an old friend had merely popped into her head.

6

She rang the doorbell.

There was no answer.

Odd. It was school holidays. The car was outside. There were nine O'Sullivan children, one of them was always hanging around the house.

She rang again. She heard the doorbell echo. A baby cried. That would be Noel, he'd be about nine months now. Eve didn't know anything about babies, but she was pretty sure they didn't stay at home alone. She looked up at the window, *his* window. She thought she caught a movement, tiny, almost imperceptible. As though someone had moved too close to a curtain as they'd stepped back, out of sight. She picked up a pebble and threw it. It clipped the window. In the silence, it sounded really loud. No-one looked out. No-one came.

She stood outside the blank closed door and suddenly she felt like an idiot, in her swanky clothes with all her makeup on, all got up, as if for a Saturday night disco. Red embarrassment started at her ankles and flamed straight up her body to her face. She turned and hurried away. She wanted to crawl into her bed and never come out. She swerved onto the path that led to the shore, no-one would see her down there. When she was little the first thing she did when they got here was to rush out and touch the sea. Now she barely looked at the waves. She had to concentrate as she tottered across the granite boulders in her wedges. When she missed her footing and slid into a rock pool she started to cry in earnest.

Eve was bedraggled when she pushed open the back door of the cottage. The twins fell about laughing.

"Yuck! You've got black on ya!" they screeched pointing at Eve's cheeks where the mascara had run in great sooty rivulets.

"There you are!" Mum was up to her elbows in the sink. Mum always did a big wash when they arrived. If she saw the mess Eve was in, she didn't say. "You can dry, there's a tea towel in the drawer. How was the beach? Tide in or out?"

Eve took a tea towel and started to dry the glasses, slowly.

"I went down to the O'Sullivans."

Mum's hands stilled momentarily. Then started on the mugs.

"How are they keeping?" she asked.

"It was weird, no-one answered the door."

"Maybe they've gone out for the day," said Mum.

"They never do that," said Eve.

Dad walked in. The salt had already got to him and his hair was curling and springing free, nothing like his everyday commuter hair.

"Who's hidden the key to the shed?" he asked.

"Eve's been to the O'Sullivans' but no-one's in," said Mum and she looked at Dad and Dad looked at her. The air pinged with questions.


"All the better for us," said Dad. His voice was rich and cheerful. "Your Mum could do with a hand and if the twins don't go down to the beach soon they'll solo-launch into space as their very own jet-propelled rockets. I'm checking the boat.

What d'you think of a morning fishing trip?"

Fishing had not been part of Eve's plan. Fishing! She wanted to be sauntering along the beach in the twilight, holding hands as she watched the sun set over the waves, skimming stones, laughing, dancing, being ... with him. Not bloody fishing.

"You like fishing," Dad said.

"I hate fishing!" She slammed the half dry mug on the counter. "Leave me alone!" She stomped out of the room.


Eve did go out fishing. Dad made her. She grumbled and complained and moaned that she was cold and wet and she hated the boat and she hated fishing and she hated the twins, of course she did, look at them pretending to be sick over the side and why did she have to come and she was going to sit completely still at the front with a tarpaulin pulled right over her because it was bloody freezing, and yes she was old enough to swear, she was fourteen for god's sake, and 'bloody' didn't count anyway. It didn't, it definitely didn't. Then the engine started and the boat chugged out into the bay and it picked up speed and it scudded over the water. She looked up from under the tarpaulin and the wind caught her in her face and the sun glittered off the tops of the waves. She took a deep breath of air.

Dad cut the engine, and pointed to ripples on the surface of the water.

"We'll try here."

He handed a fishing line each to the twins and one to Eve and she took it because what on earth else was she going to do, just sit there? She dropped the line over the side and stared down into the dark blue depths of the sea. She saw the glint of silver and felt a tug on her line –

"Got one!" she shouted and pulled it in, hand over hand, forgetting that it was not cool to be excited as she saw the iridescent scales on the muscly body thrashing on her hook.

"Look Dad!" she said as she pulled it in, "Look at the size of it!" She turned round but Dad wasn't fishing. He was looking through his binoculars, staring at the shore.

"Not as big as mine!" crowed Big Twin, so she threw her fish at him and forgot about the binoculars in the race to get more and more fish, and certainly more than the twins. Dad was right. They were over a shoal. The fish were flapping in the bottom of the boat as they dropped the lines again and again –

"Enough," said Dad. "That's plenty for us, and some left over."

He put down his binoculars, turned the boat and headed towards shore, to the spot where they always dropped the lobster pot. They hoped for lobster. They only ever got prawns.

"Down she goes," said Dad as he flung the pot over the side and Eve watched as the rope spooled out of his hands until he was only holding the pink buoy, and then he threw that into the water so it bobbed on the surface, marking their spot.

Mum admired the bucket of silvery mackerel they brought into the kitchen.

"So many!" she said. "You were lucky."

"We were skilful. We'll gut 'em and clean 'em and get 'em grill-ready," said Dad. "Come on Queen Gutter, this

*10*

is your moment."

Eve was good at gutting fish. She enjoyed the precision of it, like being a surgeon. Maybe she should *be* a surgeon, when she was grown up, as she was already so good at it? She was proud that the blood didn't make her squirm like some of her school friends did when she told them.

"Gross," they'd say and hold their noses at the thought. "Can't believe you'd do that. It's disgusting."

Eve decided that even though she was now 14, and too old for it, she would keep her title of Queen Gutter, especially as the twins were snapping at her heels, trying overthrow her. Eve took her knife, which was very sharp, and slit each fish belly. Then she thrust her thumb in, pushing the guts out to clean the cavity, rinsing it under the cold water tap until every thread of blood and sinew had gone. She could do this. She was strong, she was powerful, she could swim against the tide. She knew what she wanted and she'd fight for it. When she'd finished, the bucket slopped half full of guts and the cleaned mackerel were piled high on a plate.

"If we've got extra, can I take some over to Liam?" she said.

A missing beat. A shimmer in the air.

"Of course." Mum didn't look at her.

Eve reached under the table to the box which held old newspapers. Like the Irish Times which Dad had bought on the ferry over yesterday. She put the newspaper on the table to wrap the three mackerel. She read the headline.

"Who's Bobby Sands?" she asked, as she laid the fish on the face of a smiling young man with long wavy hair. "And what's a hunger strike?"

This time as she walked to the O'Sullivan's house she didn't stroll. She strode. The mackerel were wrapped in the newspaper, and the parcel was in a flimsy blue plastic bag. The fish bag banged against her leg as she walked. She could smell it and she knew the fish smell would linger on her hands and her leg for days, however much she scrubbed. Still. Perhaps he wouldn't notice. He'd be too distracted by the hilarity of her jokes and the bounce of her newly-conditioned hair.

When she got to the O'Sullivans' front door she did feel nervous. But she'd been to this front door so often, had been welcomed in for tea and toast, for beans, for warmth and laughter, so much laughter. The O'Sullivans were her friends.

She rang the bell. She could hear sounds inside, someone was running down the stairs.

The door opened. It was Liam. Her Liam. He'd really bulked up. 'Course he was fifteen now, but those eyelashes hadn't changed! Wasted on a boy. And blue eyes, how could she have forgotten how blue they were? She smiled.

"We got here yesterday."

His mouth screwed up at her.

"You think I don't know? We all know."

So he *had* been in his room. Watching.

"I brought your mum some fish, we caught them this morning."

She held out the newspaper package. The newspaper was wet now. The fish had seeped through. He looked at it, then at her.

"We don't want your fish." His face contorted as he looked at her. He was furious, seemed close to tears. Why?

*12*

"They're our fish anyways."

"Usually —"

"Things are different now," and he knocked the package out of her hands. It fell onto the doorstep. The newspaper unfurled, exposing the silver mackerel. Liam grabbed the newspaper, tipping the mackerel into the dirt.

"Get them filthy fish off of him!" She saw the smiling face of Bobby Sands, soaked in mackerel ooze.

"He's in the IRA," she stuttered.

"He's a hero," said Liam and he slammed indoors, taking the newspaper with him.

Eve didn't move. She couldn't. What had just happened?

She looked at the house. In the front window Mrs O'Sullivan was standing, staring out at her, her mouth a hard, straight line. Mrs O'Sullivan raised her hand, but not to wave. She pulled the curtain closed, shutting Eve out.

Eve looked at the mackerel. Grit was sticking to their scales. Their eyes were filmed with white. A fly landed on a drop of blood at the base of one feathery black fin.

Eve turned and ran, as fast as she could, to the cottage.


When she got back, she sat under the table reading newspapers. March 1st. That's when Bobby Sands first refused food, and that was over a month ago. Eve wondered what a month without food would be like. Sometimes she missed breakfast if she was particularly slow getting ready for school and by the time it was lunchtime she was famished. She prodded and pushed at her stomach to try to make it disappear.

Bobby was a prisoner in the Maze, which sounded kind of romantic and made out of yew trees, but was in fact a prison, up in Ulster, a place Eve had only heard about when she overheard the news headlines on the telly, a place where the Troubles were raging, a place of bombs and riots. Nothing to do with her. Nothing to do with here.

Only, it seemed it was to do with here.

"Mackerel supper, coming up," shouted Dad. He had lit the charcoal in the pit they used as a barbecue. He'd slotted over the grill and when it was hot, put five fat silver mackerel on it. They were sizzling and spitting, their tails curling up in the heat. Mum had laid potato salad and lettuce on the picnic table, and a bowl of lemons, cut into quarters.

"Plates please, Eve," said Dad when she arrived. He turned over the fish. Eve could see the bubbled, charred skin.

"D'you think Bobby Sands would eat mackerel if he could smell it?"

They were sitting, a freshly grilled fish in front of each person. Mum and Dad stared at her.

"It smells really tasty and if you're hungry it would be ever so hard not to give in, if you got a whiff."

Eve breathed in through her nose noisily, to demonstrate. Mum opened her mouth as though to say something, but she only took out a fish bone. She placed it carefully on the edge of her plate.

"Who's Bobby Sands?" said the Small Twin.

"He's a terrorist," said Mum.

"I wonder if they cook food outside his cell. To tempt him. D'you think they do?"

Dad was clenching his teeth.

"I mean, I'm sure he'd get off the hook if he could," she said.

She could see Dad's jaw twitching. She didn't stop.

"What do you think would be the best food to cook? To make him want to eat? Maybe he doesn't like mackerel. What about baking bread, that smells yummy. Maybe he likes burgers. Or chips!"

"Chips!" said the Big Twin.

"Chicken and chips!" said the Small Twin, because that was his favourite.

"Roast beef!" said Eve. "Oooo bacon!"

"Enough!" Dad's fist smashed down. They all jumped, the crockery rattled. "Enough. No more about Bobby Sands, not at my table."

Eve pushed her plate away.

If Bobby Sands was strong enough to stop eating, so could she.


Eve woke to the smell of bacon.

She was starving. Literally starving.

She had a moment of excitement – they were in Ireland! there was bacon! – before she remembered. The look in Liam's eyes yesterday when he saw her. As if the sight of her made him physically sick. She pushed the memory away. She'd spent so long thinking about him, dreaming about him. She couldn't give up on him now.

"Eve! Breakfast!"

She thought about heroes. About Bobby Sands in his cell in the Maze. About what she could do to prove herself worthy of Liam. To change his mind.

"Eve!"

"I'm not hungry!" she shouted.

She turned and bit her pillow, willing it to be true.


Eve waited until the smell of bacon had quite gone, and she couldn't hear the twins gobbling and shrieking in the kitchen, before she came in to pour herself a glass of milk. That would have to be enough for her breakfast.

She saw the car was gone.

"Where's Dad?" she asked.

"He's got some business," said Mum, making herself a cuppa. Eve noticed she added an extra lump of sugar. Must be for her nerves. Mum did suffer with her nerves.

"What kind of business?" asked Eve. Dad never worked when they were here. Here was for fun, family, adventure.

"Oh, leave it off for one minute, can't you, Evie?" said Mum. She gathered the plates together and crashed them into the sink.

Eve was taken aback. She hadn't even been trying to be annoying.

Later that morning, Eve was doing a What Kind of Sinner Are You? quiz in *Honey* when Mum came into her room.

"We need bread so I've got to go into the village," said Mum. "We can walk, it's not far."

"I'll stay here," said Eve.

"I'd like you to come," said Mum.

"I've got a tummy ache."

"I need you to —

"I don't want to!"

"You're coming." Eve opened her mouth to protest but Mum held up her hand. "I don't want to leave you on your own."

Eve was so surprised she just nodded. Weird, Eve thought, as she pulled on her plimsols. They'd been coming to the cottage since she was a toddler. She was allowed freedom here that she was never allowed back in the English suburbs. Then she realised. The way to the village went past Liam's house. She wasn't ready to see him yet.

"Can we walk along the beach?" she said. There'd be less chance of being spotted on the beach. Mum looked at her. Eve hadn't told Mum what had happened with Liam and his mother. She saw she didn't need to.

"Of course," said Mum.

At the Mace store in the village Mum bought sliced white bread, a cabbage and two packets of pink sausages. Eve loitered at the news stand. Bobby Sands' face was on the front page of every paper. Day 36, they shouted in large black newsprint. 36 days without food. 18% of his body weight would be lost. He'd be suffering loss of hearing, loss of vision. Organ failure would start to set in.

"I'm done," called Mum.

"Coming," Eve called back. She took one copy of each of the papers to the cashier.

"These please." It was Jamie Doyle behind the counter. She'd been on a bike ride with his brother last year, spent days swimming with him and Liam off the headland. Jamie didn't meet her eye. She gave him a five punt note. He slammed the change on the counter. She felt like she was buying pornography.

Mum took the Small Twin by the hand and Eve took the Big Twin by the hand and they walked back through the village. An old man was sitting outside Michael Shea's pub. As they passed him, Eve heard a hiss. Faint but sure. She glanced at Mum. Mum's eyes were fixed ahead. They were walking fast. Faster. Eve wanted to run. She was scared. She started to trot.

"No," said Mum, voice low. "No. Back straight, eyes forward. Walk."

The hissing was louder now. There was a face at a window. A man at a bus stop. Why had the village become so long? A child peered out of an alleyway. They had to get beyond the church. Eve was sweating. The palm of her hand was slippery. She clutched at the Big Twin's hand harder.

"Owww," he wailed and tried to pull his hand away.

"Shut it," she said and there must have been something in how she said it because he did and he kept up with them until they had left the church behind and there was just the cawing of the gulls and the *whishh whishh* of the waves and they slowed right down and Eve could feel Mum relaxing, a little bit.

When they got to the shore path they both automatically took it. So that they didn't have to walk past the O'Sullivans' house.

When they got back to the cottage the relief was palpable.

Mum got out the flapjacks she'd made yesterday. The twins took two each and she didn't stop them. She offered the tin to Eve. Eve shook her head.

"It won't work, you know," said Mum and she looked at the pile of newspapers Eve had put on the table. "It won't make a difference."

Eve felt overwhelmed with fury.

"What do you know?" she said, "What do you know about anything? You're old. And you're English."

Mum gave the smallest of shrugs.

"You might not like it pet, but so are you."

"I'm Dad's daughter. He's Irish, I'm Irish. Grandpa went over the water and now Dad's come back to put down his roots. He has to be over there for work. But it's here where he belongs. Where I belong." Eve was hot in her certainty. She took the nearest newspaper and started to read. Mum came up behind her and kissed the top of her head, squeezed her shoulder. Eve shook her off.

Hallucinations. Brain damage. Vitamin deficiency leading to blindness. Muscle and tissue of the intestine shrivelling, leading to profuse diarrhoea. The body absorbing muscle to feed itself, including the heart muscle, leading to heart failure. Disappearance of the diaphragm, leading to inability to breath. There were no reports of how Bobby's body was responding, or not in these newspapers. But Eve's stomach felt like it had been gutted. Scooped out, like those mackerel. And it was only 12 o'clock.

Eve couldn't believe that Dad didn't notice the minute he walked in the door that everyone had gone mad. He got back at six. The twins were ricocheting off the walls. They were kicking a ball around the kitchen and were about to break something and launch Mum into her third rage of the afternoon. The rain had set in hard and none of them could go outside. Eve didn't want to anyway and she bet Mum didn't either, not after their morning walk. Eve thought about reading *Honey* or *Just Seventeen* but she couldn't. They were too trivial after what she'd read in the newspaper. She didn't care about mascara anymore, or how to individualise her jeans by sewing on applique patches. She was serious now, political. She wondered whether, if she was in prison, she'd be brave enough to write a diary and secrete it in a body cavity. She wondered what body cavity Bobby Sands used. She decided that she'd start a diary in her notebook but Mum said she had to play monopoly as it was no good with just three. They'd played monopoly for hours and the Big Twin had won which made Eve teary which would not normally happen and which made the Big Twin give her a sticky hug, which she didn't like. The twins were having a football break before their supper when Dad walked in.

Eve saw he'd smoothed down his hair. He looked tired. Mum took him out of the kitchen and Eve could hear them have a whispered conversation in the hall.

Dad burst back into the kitchen.

"Right kiddos!" his voice was big and booming and Holiday Dad was back. "We're going to the pub."

Eve loved it when they went to pubs. They only ever went when they were here. She loved sitting outside in the gardens with the palm trees, so weird, it was like they were somewhere really hot when actually they weren't at all. She liked eating crisps and Dad letting her have a sip of his *Guinness*. But on this visit everything was different.

She looked at Mum. Mum had been in the village. Mum knew what had happened. But Mum was smiling and nodding.

Perhaps it would be all right.


They all piled into the car and instead of going towards the village, they went the other way, to the other village, which was a bit further. A bit more private perhaps.

Mum took Eve and the twins straight into the garden. They found a table where they could all watch the boats scudding across the bay. Dad went in to order.


Then Dad was hurrying out of the back door of the bar carrying a tray. He was balancing two pints of *Guinness* and three cokes, with a pile of crisp packets. He was trying to stop the drinks sloshing on his packet of *Marlboros*.

Right behind him came Mick O'Sullivan, Liam's dad, and the three oldest O'Sullivan boys. Pat. Cormac. And, Eve saw, Liam. They were mid-conversation and Mick was not being friendly.

"What are you doing for her? Your mistress, Mrs Bloody Thatcher?" shouted Mick.

"I'm not –"

"Y'are. We know what you do, we know who you are. That's why you're here, having a 'holiday'." Mick's fingers made the air quote expression and his face contorted into a sneer. "Isn't it? Isn't it!"

"I do work for the government it's true –"

"The *British* government!"

"But –"

"His blood! His blood will be on your hands!"


Eve realised she was holding her breath. Then she saw that Liam had come and was standing right close to her. He must want to speak to her, mustn't he?

"Liam. Liam! I've read all about Bobby Sands. I think…I think it's wonderful what he's doing. I support it. All of it. So I'm…I've stopped eating Liam, in solidarity with him."

She was proud of the word 'solidarity'. It sounded so grown up.

Eve wondered later what she'd thought he'd do.

Sweep her into his arms?

Tell her that he loved her?

That he admired and respected what she was doing?

But what he said was:

"You? Solidarity?"

Then Liam turned, strode up to Dad, put his fists together and whacked the tray out of his hands and into Dad's body.

The *Guinness* dripped off Dad's trousers and the glasses smashed on the ground.

"Why don't you all fuck off back to England?" Liam shouted.

And Mick O'Sullivan spat, spat at Dad, full in his face.

Eve watched as the spittle dripped from his cheek. Mum ran to him, and took her hankie to wipe it off.


Eve thought of how excited Dad always was when they set off for Ireland, his joy when they arrived. She thought of him digging in the cottage garden, the black earth that he knew was his, wrenching out the boulders that formed the backbone of the land. She thought of how he always said they must be proud of their heritage, proud of their Irish roots. How he spun them tales, of the giant Finn McCool and the Children of Lir, of High King Brian Boru and Niall of the Nine Hostages, the stories of Old Ireland. She didn't know what this job of his was. But she did know that he said he was just passing time in England. That soon they would move here, move back, move home.


It was overwhelming.

Eve fainted.

She opened her eyes. Dad was staring down at her.

"She's not eaten today, or last night. It's the hunger that's done it," said Mum

And Liam leant over, his face contorted.

"It's not about the hunger, you eejit. It's about the cause."

"That's enough now," said Dad. "Leave her alone!"

"You're not fit to lick his boots," snarled Liam and he turned his back.

The cause. Getting the English out of Ireland.

Where did that leave her?


Their car headlights lit up the cottage. Eve saw that eggs had been thrown at the front door. A yolk was stuck by the door handle and egg whites smeared the paint.

She was not surprised. Nothing would surprise her right now.

Dad turned off the ignition and sagged.

Mum put her hand over his. She leant in and kissed his cheek.

After a moment he said. "We'll pack up. Drive to Cork. Take the night ferry to Fishguard."

There was silence in the car.

The Small Twin started to sniff.

It was Mum who spurred them to action.

"Come on, let's race! The winner is the one who can

pack up quickest!" She clapped her hands. "Chop chop!" she said.

The Big Twin was out of the car and up the path to the back door first and even Eve felt a twinge of excitement as she clambered out. Then she swayed.

"Mum," she said. "Can I have a flapjack?"


It didn't take long to pack the car with suitcases and food and bedding and shoes and fishing rods and anoraks. Dad locked up and put the key under the stone. They drove out of the cottage gates, through the village and away, singing 'She'll be Coming O'er The Mountain When She Comes' at the tops of their voices as they set off, for home.


Bobby Sands died on May 5th 1981. He'd been on hunger strike for 65 days. By that time, Eva was back at school, spinning tales to Becca of how she'd told a boy with blue blue eyes where to get off 'cos she wasn't gonna take any of his cheek. She didn't even see the news.


Eve never went to the cottage again. The next year, the family went on holiday to France. If any of the French boys asked her where she was from:


"I'm English," she'd say. "Through and through."

# Author Biography

Clare Reddaway is a Bath-based writer of short stories and plays. Her short stories have been widely published online (*Barren Magazine, Fictive Dream, Fairlight Books, Storgy Magazine, Blue Nib*) and in anthologies (Fairlight Book of Short Stories 2020, Aesthetica Creative Writing Annual 2020, Bath Short Story Anthology, Momaya Short Story Review).

Last year she was shortlisted for the Bridport Prize, having previously won and been shortlisted for many other national competitions.

Her work is frequently broadcast on BBC Radio Bristol and local community radio stations, and she has had stories recorded by Tempest Productions for their Unbound podcast.

Her plays have been staged across the UK. She is currently developing a play *Flotsam* with Theatre West, and a screenplay *Whale Song* with Screenology in Bristol.

She runs regular live lit events in Bath (Story Fridays, Stories At The Farm, Festive Doorstep Stories). She often writes site-specific stories which she either performs on location (for instance at a derelict Georgian lido in Bath), or as story walks.

She is currently compiling a short story collection and brooding on a potential novella. She has an MA in Creative Writing from Bath Spa University.

Find out more at www.clarereddaway.co.uk.

**Social Media:**

Twitter: @CReddaway

# Enjoy the rest of our 2021 Shorts Season:

## Pigskin by David Hartley

Something strange is happening to the animals on the farm.

A pig becomes bacon, chickens grow breadcrumbs, a cow turns to leather, a goat excretes cheese. As food becomes scarce and the looming 'pot-bellies' threaten to invade the safety of the sty, Pig knows he must get to the bottom of this strange phenomenon or face imminent death. Reminiscent of Animal Farm and darkly satirical, David Hartley interrogates the ethics of farming and the potential problems of genetic

engineering, asking important questions about our

relationship to the food – or animals – we eat.

*"Pigskin is a knife-sharp, knowing fable about animal instincts and human ingenuity. David Hartley has a gift for creating stories that leave scars."*

- Aliya Whiteley, author of The Loosening Skin

## PowerPoint Eulogy by Mark Wilson

Three corporate hours have been allotted to commemorate the life of enigma, Bill Motluck. Employee memories of his life are crudely recounted onto a dusty projector. No one has ever been quite sure of his purpose. No one is quite sure who wrote the PowerPoint…but it seems to be exposing them all, one by one.

*"In his wildly imaginative chapbook, PowerPoint Eulogy, Chicago writer and visual artist Mark Wilson paints a picture of corporate culture—and humanity at large—that is both soul-crushingly bleak and hilariously demented. Divided into forty-four presenta-*

tion "slides", the story centers on the memories a group of unnamed employees have of their recently deceased co-worker, Bill Motluck—a man so bland he enjoyed small talk about skim milk, and so desperate to fit in he once rented a newborn for Bring Your Kid to Work Day. Should we give in to the impulse to laugh at poor Bill, or feel sympathy for his plight? As the stories and little revelations pile up, it becomes harder and harder to decide—and the tension this creates is what ultimately makes this one-of-a-kind collection so impossible to put down. I laughed, I winced, I loved it".

- Mark Rader, Author of 'The Wanting Life'.

## Muscle and Mouth by Louise Finnigan

*"A beautifully written and compelling story"*

- Kerry Hudson, Award-Winning Author of 'Lowborn'

*"Muscle and Mouth made me feel the fracture of my own northern identity deep in my gut. It made me ache for home. It reminded me that leaving a place means giving pieces of yourself away; your rawness, your language and a certain kind of love. Louise Finnigan is a writer to watch."*

- Jessica Andrews, Author of 'Saltwater' and Winner of 2020 Portico Prize

Jade is prepping an A-Level assignment, all her sights set on Durham University. She's told she has to 'prove herself' and keep her away from the unsavoury types she calls her best friends. Yet Jade is reluctant to shun her corner of Manchester, where she finds the land rich, 'dark with energy'.

## Hassan's Zoo by Ruth Brandt

*Hassan's Zoo*

When American soldiers invade Iraq searching for weapons of mass destruction, Kesari the Bengal tiger and other wildlife are at the mercy of guns and keeper, Hassan.

Entrenched in perpetual fear, Hassan must exercise Godly powers over his creatures in his attempts to save them - and himself.

*A Village in Winter*

"Mrs Gregory said to leave Frizz and his mum be for a while. Stop pestering. That poor woman with that lad."

In the chill of winter, the villagers play by the river, their play as harsh as the ice.


## How To Bring Him Back by Claire HM

*'If I was going to cast a spell tonight, this night of a full arse moon as stark and crunchy as a ten-day crust of snow, I'd start by telling the earth to spin in the opposite direction.*

*By what power?*

*By the power of my pen.'*

'How to Bring Him Back' is a journey into a darkly humorous love triangle. It's 90s Birmingham and Cait is post-university, aimless and working in a dive bar. She's caught between Stadd, who's stable, funny, compatible as a friend, and her compulsive sexual attraction with Rik. Present day Cait picks up her pen, on her yearly writing retreat to Aberystwyth, and addresses an absent Stadd with the lessons she has learnt from her past.

## About Fly on the Wall Press

A publisher with a conscience.
Publishing high quality anthologies on pressing issues,
chapbooks and poetry products, from exceptional poets
around the globe.
Founded in 2018 by founding editor, Isabelle Kenyon.

## Other publications:

*Please Hear What I'm Not Saying*

*Persona Non Grata*

*Bad Mommy / Stay Mommy by Elisabeth Horan*

*The Woman With An Owl Tattoo by Anne Walsh Donnelly*

*the sea refuses no river by Bethany Rivers*

*White Light White Peak by Simon Corble*

*Second Life by Karl Tearney*

*The Dogs of Humanity by Colin Dardis*

*Small Press Publishing: The Dos and Don'ts by Isabelle Kenyon*

*Alcoholic Betty by Elisabeth Horan*

*Awakening by Sam Love*

*Grenade Genie by Tom McColl*

*House of Weeds by Amy Kean and Jack Wallington*

*No Home In This World by Kevin Crowe*

*The Goddess of Macau by Graeme Hall*

*The Prettyboys of Gangster Town by Martin Grey*

*The Sound of the Earth Singing to Herself by Ricky Ray*

*Inherent by Lucia Orellana Damacela*

*Medusa Retold by Sarah Wallis*

*Pigskin by David Hartley*

*We Are All Somebody*

*Aftereffects by Jiye Lee*

*Someone Is Missing Me by Tina Tamsho-Thomas*

*Odd as F*ck by Anne Walsh Donnelly*

*Muscle and Mouth by Louise Finnigan*

*Modern Medicine by Lucy Hurst*

*These Mothers of Gods by Rachel Bower*

*Andy and the Octopuses by Isabelle Kenyon*

*Sin Is Due To Open In A Room Above Kitty's by Morag Anderson*

*Fauna by Dr. David Hartley*

*No One Has Any Intention Of Building A Wall by Ruth Brandt*

## Social Media:

@fly_press (Twitter)

@flyonthewall_poetry (Instagram)

@flyonthewallpress (Facebook)

www.flyonthewallpress.co.uk